THE HAPPY READER

A READER READING

The Jardin des Tuileries is one of the most reader-friendly outdoor spaces in the world. There are countless chairs on which to perch, all in thrall to an ornate octagonal pool. Map-clutching travellers ogle the historic statues. Delegates stroll, en route from the National Assembly, just across the Seine, to the excellent Japanese restaurants near Pyramides. Art lovers linger in the north-west corner, by the Galerie Nationale du Jeu de Paume. And everywhere, because this is a beautiful park at the centre of a great city of readers, there are people with books. Paris is home to more than seven hundred bookshops, many of them tiny, independent caverns of paper with mysterious specialities like 'realism' or 'Eurasian travel'. This reader may have been photographed in 1957, but the chairs remain the same, and his equivalent is 100% definitely sat on one of them today. Welcome, then, to issue 2 of *The Happy Reader*, a magazinified version of a brilliant park in which to read.

Issue nº 2 — Spring 2015

The Happy Reader is
a collaboration between
Penguin Classics and
Fantastic Man

EDITOR-IN-CHIEF
Seb Emina

EDITORIAL DIRECTORS
Jop van Bennekom
Gert Jonkers

MANAGING EDITOR
Cecilia Stein

DESIGN
Jop van Bennekom
Helios Capdevila
Matthew Young

PRODUCTION
James Blackman

PUBLISHER
Stefan McGrath

MARKETING DIRECTOR
Nicola Hill

BRAND MANAGER
Sam Voulters

PICTURE RESEARCH
Rebecca Moldenhauer

CONTRIBUTORS
Jason Evans, Clym Evernden, Max Farago, Marius W. Hansen, Henry Jeffreys, Roland Kelts, Jeff Koehler, Kacper Lasota, Yann Le Bec, Nicholas Lezard, Damian Noszkowicz, Megan Wray Schertler, Noel Smith, Sadie Stein, Alexis Taylor, Thomas Chatterton Williams.

THANK YOU
Magnus Åkesson, Zac Bayly, Jill Crawford, Lauren Elkin, Andy Extance, Linda Fallon, Jordan Kelly, Alicia Kirby, Rebecca Lee, Penny Martin, Tom Meanwell, Anna Mears, Abeku Nelson, Dan Papps, Caroline Pretty, Adrian Read.

Penguin Books
80 Strand
London WC2R 0RL

info@thehappyreader.com
www.thehappyreader.com

SNIPPETS

Tidings, whispers, events and curios to gladden the vernal bookworm.

LOVELY — At a bookshop in Atlanta airport, an elderly woman held up *Fifty Shades of Grey* and said to another customer, in a quiet Southern accent, 'I hear this is a lovely book.'

*

THINKETH — Justin Bieber was spotted with the 1902 self-help book *As a Man Thinketh*. But why? Its author, James Allen, wanted to show readers how 'they themselves are the makers of themselves', which is no doubt a pleasing way of thinking about those 14m album sales and 3.75bn YouTube views. Or perhaps it was for lyrical inspiration: Funkadelic's 'Good Thoughts, Bad Thoughts' was based on it. Who knows! He may never sayeth.

*

PROMISE — One of the big innovative trends of the year is the website that automatically sends you everyday items, such as socks, when you're running low. All very clever and modern, but also strangely familiar. A character in Justin Cartwright's 2004 novel *The Promise of Happiness* made his fortune from precisely such an online sock business.

*

SPRITZ — Parisian English-language bookshop Shakespeare and Company is, for the first time, selling books online, and it's far from the average e-commerce initiative. Customers can select from a range of characterful extras to go with their book delivery, including a spritz of perfume that smells like Paris (though hopefully not certain bits of the Metro), and a love poem tapped out on an Underwood typewriter by one of the so-called 'tumbleweeds' — wayward souls who help out at the shop in return for being able to sleep there.

SNIPPETS

FACEBOOK — Grammy-nominated singer FKA twigs, not in the mood to have her photo taken on Miami Beach, covered her face with the closest object to hand — a book. Her lens-blocker was Anaïs Nin's short story collection *Delta of Venus*, including, aptly enough, a tale called 'The Veiled Woman'.

*

MYSTERY — Pennsylvania's largest bookshop dedicated to the mystery genre is up for sale. Mystery Lovers' outgoing owner says it's all been going well, but she just doesn't have the time. Case closed.

*

MIDFIELD — The National Literacy Trust, a UK charity, has appointed footballer Frank Lampard as its new ambassador. The Manchester City midfield ace is an avid reader, and the author of ten books including *Totally Frank: The Autobiography of Frank Lampard* and *Frankie's Magic Football: Frankie vs The Rowdy Romans*.

RED ALL OVER — Former Washington Post reporter Ellen Crosby is having considerable success with novels combining wine with crime, such as *The Riesling Retribution* and *The Vintage Vendetta*. What next? *Merlot, She Wrote*? *The Name of the Rosé*?

*

LOUCHE — Bibliophiles will note a familiar face at the London International Antiquarian Book Fair in May. The man behind Neil Pearson Rare Books is none other than *that* Neil Pearson, the sitcom stalwart also known for his roles in films such as *Bridget Jones's Diary* and *Fever Pitch*. Appropriately for an actor known for playing louche womanisers, one of his specialities is rare erotica. His most expensive item? One of Aleister Crowley's original notebooks, snap-uppable at the time of writing for £12,500.

*

B'SHOP — The former Archbishop of Canterbury, Rowan Williams, is a regular in a London station bookshop. He usually buys current affairs magazine *Private Eye*. A bookseller, wishing to alert her colleagues to his presence without saying anything out loud, wrote down 'archbishop' on a slip of paper. Much to everyone's, especially Rowan's, embarrassment, her colleague responded by shouting 'Archbishop? Who's the archbishop?!'

*

SEXY — Fans of Stoya will be delighted to hear that the popular pornographic actress is currently writing a semi-memoiristic novel about the adult entertainment industry, which will cover its ethics, politics, economics and history since the 1980s. The 28-year-old from Wilmington, North Carolina, who has won several Adult Video News Awards including Hottest Sex Scene and Best All-Girl Group Sex Scene, has previously written for *Esquire*, *Vice* and the esteemed *New York Times* newspaper.

KIM GORDON

As co-founder, bassist, guitarist and vocalist for Sonic Youth, Kim Gordon is alternative rock royalty, but that barely scratches the surface of her résumé. The New York-born, LA-raised Gordon is an accomplished visual artist who exhibits regularly, produced Hole's breakthrough album *Pretty on the Inside* and co-directed The Breeders' 'Cannonball' video, appeared in the Gus Van Sant movie *Last Days* and launched a range of skatewear, and whose list of collaborators — Raymond Pettibon, Marc Jacobs, Carrie Brownstein — reads like a contemporary *Who's Who*. For these and so many other reasons, her just-released memoir, *Girl in a Band*, is nigh-on impossible to put down.

In conversation with
SADIE STEIN

Portraits by
MAX FARAGO

KIM GORDON

KIM GORDON
(28-04-53)

Born in Rochester, New York. Raised in Los Angeles. Studied at Otis Art Institute of Los Angeles County. Bands include: CKM, Sonic Youth, Free Kitten, Harry Crews, Body/Head. Movie appearances include: *Last Days*, *I'm Not There*. Fashion projects include: X-Girl, Mirror/Dash. Mother to: Coco Hayley Gordon Moore (born 01-07-94). Dogs' names: Syd Barrett, Merzbow. Lives in: New York, Los Angeles and Northampton, Massachusetts

THE HAPPY READER

LOS ANGELES, NEW YORK

At the end of my time with Kim Gordon, at a chic coffee shop in Echo Park, LA, a friend comes to meet me. She doesn't know who I've been interviewing, and I see her eyes widen as I introduce them. 'Next time I'm going to meet the coolest woman in the world,' my friend says to me afterwards, 'give me some warning!'

For many of us, that's exactly who Kim Gordon is, a status she's held for the past thirty-plus years. When we meet up, Gordon is about to kick off a Body/Head tour. Although her schedule is crazy with photo shoots and appointments, Gordon, at sixty-one, is unruffled and casually chic. She has that innate California chillness, and the quiet confidence of someone with nothing to prove. Her stories are filled with unselfconscious references to Steven, to Sofia, to Chloe, but it's the furthest thing from name-dropping; it's her life.

Since splitting with husband and Sonic Youth co-founder Thurston Moore in 2011, Gordon has weathered media scrutiny and personal upheaval with characteristic sangfroid, and if anything her status as a thinking feminist's icon has been strengthened. In 2012 she founded noise duo Body/Head with Bill Nace, and her memoir, *Girl in a Band*, has just been released worldwide.

So, yes, she's a towering cultural phenomenon. But here's the thing: Gordon is also *nice*. She's easy company and a great listener. Unpretentious to the point of self-deprecation, she's interested in everything and totally free of intellectual snobbery. Even though she's read a lot, and knows a lot, she's quick to disclaim any expertise, and is as eager for your opinion as to give her own — more so. Here's how unintimidating she is: after I take a wrong turn down an alley, en route to a different building where the cafe's bathroom is meant to be, and accidentally use the bathroom in the house of a *stranger* who then questions me on my way out, I come back to the table and can't resist telling her, and we laugh our heads off. But then, that's exactly how the coolest woman in the world *would* react.

SADIE: You grew up around here. Does California still feel like home to you?

KIM: In a way it does. My friends always say I seem most relaxed here. And just being around the familiar terrain, and smells... even this place where I'm staying, it has such a distinct California smell. I tried to write about it, but I don't know if I really captured it. A little bit of gas, and not quite a musty smell, but a little dry and a little damp, mixed together. Night-blooming jasmine, butterfly bush, eucalyptus. Just knowing the names of the trees. I hardly know any names of trees on the east coast. I know what a maple tree is *(laughs)*.

S: It reminds me of the way Joan Didion describes California in *Where I Was From*.

K: You know what? I actually hadn't read Didion until a couple of years ago. I mean, I'd read some, but not deeply. It was a name that always was around. Then when Lizzy Goodman interviewed me in *Elle* she described me as being Joan Didion-esque or something, and I thought, *Wow, she really got me!* I mean, it's the California thing. Then I went back and I read *The White Album*. I haven't read her latest, really depressing things. But what I like is that she's in some ways not explicitly female — at least, she's not girlish. She was in some ways writing in this man's world, in Hollywood, but she's pointing out things that wouldn't be pointed out otherwise. I never really thought about what gender a voice has in writing. It's not that she writes like a man, but it's just that she writes like a really interesting woman! Actually, my friend said about Donna Tartt that she writes like a gay man. I said, well, that's really interesting... I don't know, what's your take on Didion's voice?

S: I've always liked her combination of remove, and cool intellect, and the willingness to be egocentric when necessary. And speaking of being in a man's world — the way she took advantage of being overlooked, of moving under the radar. But that's not unlike the 'girl with the band' phenomenon that you get into in your memoir.

K: Right, in that you're allowed to be a voyeur, an observer. I like the idea of just working from a point of weakness. That can be a shield in itself, in a way.

S: Do you feel like, in terms of gender dynamics — for lack of a better phrase — your daughter's entering a different world?

K: Possibly. I think Coco probably takes for granted a lot of things about the world, because she doesn't know any different. But she does have a confidence — at least outwardly — that I never did. Maybe it's also being an only child. I mean, there's nothing like the attitude of a teenage girl. I love that movie *Ghost World*. Coco and her friend Addie would work at this record store during the summer, and they would just sit there exuding so much attitude, playing computer games, giving people little pieces of false information about collector records. I wanted to make a film about them — *Ghost World 2* or

1. GHOST WORLD
—
Based on the cult comic book by Daniel Clowes, the movie *Ghost World* (pictured) is not about ghosts at all, but the lives of two American teenagers. Clowes has said the title came from some graffiti he saw in Chicago.

something. There's a gloriousness about those years. I mean, it can be miserable, as I recall — I didn't like it — but it's a great time.

S: What were you into reading as a teenager?

K: I had an older brother who was a super-reader, and I'd read what he was reading. He became a scholar. He ended up getting his master's in Classics. He's a paranoid schizophrenic, but maybe part of his illness is that he could recite an incredible amount. Chaucer, Baudelaire... and he wrote sonnets. That's how I started reading Jean-Paul Sartre and Nietzsche, and probably D.H. Lawrence. I was really into D.H. Lawrence, because he wrote about sensuality. It was my way of rebelling against high school.

S: Did your parents mind your reading Nietzsche as a kid?

K: I don't know, but I was super-annoying. Out loud in the car, on a car trip, I'd quote *Thus Spoke Zarathustra* just to be annoying. Mostly as a way to say, *Your life is so conventional*. I was pretty bad.

S: Teenagers are supposed to do that! Since you're a musician, I wonder: were you read to as a kid? Hearing books is such a different experience to reading them.

K: I remember loving the Dr Seuss books — *Green Eggs and Ham* — and I'm sure my mother read more to me, but what I remember is that I had these records, these recordings, that I would listen to. *Winnie the Pooh* and also *Sleeping Beauty* and *Snow White*. I loved those, and I would listen to them endlessly. I would listen to records the way kids today watch videos. Oh, there was one book from my childhood that I'm sure my mom read to me: *The Lonely Doll*. I was haunted by it — I'm still haunted by those images.

S: There's that crazy biography of the author, *The Secret Life of the Lonely Doll: The Search for Dare Wright*.

K: I haven't read the whole thing. I've read excerpts, about her mom. For many years, I'd forgotten the book, who'd written it. But it really formed my ideas of New York, what the Upper East Side looked like. I was obsessed with that sort of interior. And it probably even made me want to be wealthy. *(laughs)* I lost track of it for years. And then one day my friend Julie was over. Thurston came home and he'd spotted a mock-up of one of the Lonely Doll books being sold on the street, and he'd bought it. Julie and I were both like, 'Oh my God, it's that book!' And then shortly after that, the biography came out. There was an article in the paper about all the women — like Cindy Sherman, and a lot of other people — who'd been influenced by that book. It was so funny. It's such a visual book — and so creepy! I tried

2. ANNOYING

'What child hath not reason to weep over its parents?' would, for example, be an irritating Zarathustra quote on such a car trip.

3. GREEN EGGS AND HAM

This rhyming story, published in 1960, about definitely not liking green eggs and ham, was recently rewritten in its entirety by Sarah Palin for a reading at a conservative conference. 'I do not like this Uncle Sam,' went her version, 'I do not like this health care scam.' The original ended with the narrator changing his mind.

4. WOW

Dare Wright's *The Lonely Doll* (1957) was controversial for its portrayal of its hero, Edith, who is a doll, being spanked by teddy bears. Not controversial enough, however, to prevent eighteen sequels from being published, including *The Lonely Doll Learns a Lesson* (1961) and *Edith & Big Bad Bill* (1968).

to read it to my daughter, and was just like — wow. The doll being spanked, the threat of their going away and leaving her...

S: The cross-dressing! I found it really lurid, too, because I was never spanked.

K: I wasn't either. It's almost like 'playing doctor'. The whole relationship between the doll and the bears, and something about the pink gingham...

S: The doll is oddly glamorous.

K: She was *so* glamorous. I think it was my first exposure to glamour.

S: Are you a fan of books on tape? Especially given those records you loved as a kid.

K: I should listen to more. Especially because I do so much driving; I just never get around to downloading them. I got the audiobook of *Just Kids*, but it was just too much Patti. It was too stylised for me. The flowery writing became too much in her voice. Actually, I had to read my own book for the audio version.

S: Oh, wow. Did you want to?

K: I'm sure if I hadn't wanted to, they wouldn't have made me. It's probably better, though, for a memoir, to hear the author read it. It's weird. I was just, like, this is so boring. But there were mistakes that we found, that I'd missed reading over the galleys.

S: Did you experience the text differently? Had you already read it aloud?

K: No, I'm not really into readings. But I found it interesting, because you read *everything*: even the copyright info! It's pretty funny. It's hard.

S: But, audio versions aside, you enjoy reading other people's memoirs?

K: The Mary Karr book, *The Liars' Club*, started the whole memoir, non-fiction thing for me. I had to keep reminding myself it wasn't fiction. It was so great. A lot of them I find boring. I skim them. But I haven't been reading any while I was writing. I didn't want to be influenced. There are some I'm excited about. I hear Joni Mitchell's writing a memoir. I know two people who've interviewed her, because she's put out this multi-CD box set — I just ordered it on Amazon — and she said that the existing books about her are silly, and inaccurate, so she's going to do her own.

"You know, I'm not academic or intellectual. I'm the kind of person that skims a philosophy article looking for lyric ideas."

S: Have you read either of Marianne Faithfull's memoirs?

K: I haven't, actually; I want to. I hear *Faithfull* is amazing. I hear it's the best book on the Stones. But, to be so stoned, how could she possibly remember?

S: Whether or not it's totally accurate, it feels honest! You believe it's certainly how she remembers it. And she doesn't try to make herself look good.

K: I sat next to her at a Marc Jacobs fashion show a number of years ago. We were talking about getting older, and she said, 'Well, God, we should just be thankful we're alive!' I was like, speak for yourself! But she's amazing. And her new book, of images, is so beautiful. Oh, I just remembered: I also read the Keith Richards memoir *Life*.

S: What did you think?

K: I think his ghostwriter did a really great job. I got bored during the whole Jamaica thing, but I liked hearing about his early years growing up, and everything about him and Anita was fascinating. The stuff about his son Marlon on tour — that part where he has to wake him up, and there's a gun... I read that passage to my daughter, so she wouldn't feel bad about what we put her through touring with Sonic Youth!

S: Your daughter's at the Art Institute of Chicago at the moment, right?

K: Yeah. I feel bad, because she's home in Northampton for break, and I'm missing her. She'll have to go back to Chicago before I get back.

S: Is she liking it?

K: I think she finds it scary! Much more than New York. And it's cold. The school's hard; she has to take a lot of required classes in addition to studio time. She likes literature and history but will do anything to get out of math. She's, like, taking forensics. But she's a good painter, and she's doing well. I think she'll probably do graduate work back in New York. I have a lot of friends who did that. Like, John Miller — he's having an opening tonight. He's also such a good writer. He's a great art writer.

S: Do you read a lot of art writing?

K: No, not really. I just don't have time. You know, I'm the kind of person that skims a philosophy article looking for lyric ideas (*laughs*). And I like getting excited by ideas, but I'm not academic or intellectual.

S: I don't know that I'd want to meet anyone who described themselves as intellectual!

K: Someone like Branden Joseph, though, he's a cool nerd — that's the only way I know how to describe him. What he's interested in is what makes him cool: his deep knowledge of music. I so respect people like him who can write at that level. I could never write like that, in a critical capacity.

S: It's a completely different skill-set. As you say, there's so little time to keep up with things. Do you read any periodicals or websites regularly?

K: I read *The New Yorker* and *Artforum* occasionally. I just find it hard to find time. Except on an airplane.

S: I wanted to ask you about plane reading.

K: Well, I usually start with *Us Weekly* (*laughs*). I read *Vanity Fair*. Lately, I'm really into Jo Nesbø. On tour, I started getting into noir, pulpy crime mysteries. You need something that can just pull your attention in. It's exhausting when you're travelling all the time, to keep focused. *The Killer Inside Me* by Jim Thompson made a big impression on me. I was just starting to read a lot of mysteries, getting away from hard criticism and heavy books. Storyline — which is great — aside, I liked his writing style because it's so performative and so visual. I liked the way he builds on these minimal sentences. He's in that noir tradition of Raymond Chandler, building a mood in a subtle way. So, yeah, if I'm at an airport and I need a book, I'll gravitate towards that sort of thing. Also, part of the reason I like books like Nesbø's is that you learn about other places. My friend, who's a writer, was saying that there are almost no real fiction books any more; all fiction books are filled with so much information now. So, I've learned a lot about Nazis and Norway and stuff, and just different cultures. One of Nesbø's books, *The Snowman*, takes place in Bergen, and Bill and I finally went there on tour, and I was like, oh my God! Now I know what he's talking about! It's a really cool town, but I would never have even thought of wanting to go there, if I hadn't read that.

S: I read somewhere that it's primarily women who like violent things: true crime, and also TV shows like *Law and Order: Special Victims Unit*.

5. US WEEKLY

Us Weekly is a New York City-based gossip magazine reaching an audience of 13.5 million. On average, a woman reading *Us Weekly* has a yearly income of around $77,000. She is likely to have received college education (68%), be married (47%) and have at least one child (54%).

6. COOL

Bergen is Norway's second most populous city and is located on the peninsula of Bergenshalvoyen. If a city's cool correlates with its music festival quota then, with a yearly count of ten, it certainly makes the grade. Two of these are fully dedicated to metal music, this year featuring bands such as Dark Tranquillity, Gehenna and Hecate Enthroned.

7. JAMES ELLROY
—
When Gordon interviewed James Ellroy for a 1988 issue of SPIN magazine, she asked him if he had a dog and he replied, 'I am the dog. Mostly I listen to music and lie around on my bed brooding on things. Sex is my big obsession. I think about it all the time. I turned 40 a couple days ago and I think about it more now than when I was 16.'

K: I can't watch those shows: they're too brutal! Before I had Coco I could read more James Ellroy, more violent stuff. And I can watch something like *Game of Thrones* — which can be pretty cringey — with no problem. At least there's a lot of theatricality to distance you. But *SVU*, it's so gruesome — and so often it involves a kid. I need a little more of an escape from life than that.

S: Have you read any of the Tana French mysteries?

K: Yeah! I like those. There's a new one out now, *The Secret Place*, but it's still in hardcover. I like to see where I am in a book so I have a hard time reading on a device, but I got *The Goldfinch* in hardcover but I only got halfway through because I just didn't want to lug it around any more, so it makes sense for books like that. But yeah, I like Tana French. In general, I don't read as much as I used to. I just watch so much TV.

S: What is it about TV that you love? Is it just the easier escapism?

K: TV shows seem more flexible, in a way. Most movies seem more rigid. And it sounds like a cliché, but there *are* more good roles for women.

S: You've done guest spots now on *Gilmore Girls*, *Girls*...

K: ...and *Gossip Girl*.

S: Which all do interesting things with female characters.

K: Maybe not *Gossip Girl*.

S: So, what do you watch regularly?

K: We were totally into *Friday Night Lights*, as a family: amazing, and shooting with the hand-held camera thing somehow made it feel so realistic. And *Homeland*: I love that. It just gets more and more absorbing as the days go by. Claire Danes is amazing. Oh, and *The Affair*. That was good, though sometimes a little too slow and soap opera-y. The woman who plays the other woman, there's something about her face — the Botox or something — that I find super-repulsive, but I can't stop looking. Neither character is likeable, so it's interesting. I read a really good interview with the woman who writes it.

S: Any reality shows?

K: Not really. If my daughter's watching *The Kardashians*, I'll check in on it. And I'm always just amazed. It's just like, this is so fucking boring. They're not doing anything! I will occasionally watch a show like that on an airplane, but it's all so fake. And people are starting to change their idea of what reality is, model their ideas of how you're supposed to interact with people, on those shows. That's the scariest thing to me, that they're influencing behaviour.

S: Have you seen *Nashville*?

K: I watch that because of the Connie Britton tie-in. But I think the music is actually pretty good, and it's usually not good. They can all sing, and there's a really good-looking guy: he's like the older, Tim Riggins-ish character, who's Connie Britton's long-time beau. Oh, and of course I watch *The Good Wife*.

S: So good.

K: I did an interview yesterday with someone who was going to interview Julianna Margulies, who plays the lead, afterwards. I feel so close to her *(laughs)*.

S: Lawyer friends tell me that, as these things go, it's relatively realistic.

K: It has a good tension, great characters. And I'm always curious about the older woman, Christine Baranski: what is she wearing? How is she dressed as a professional older woman? I mean, it's not the way I would ever dress, but it's so interesting to see how they dress her, how they think about things.

S: You're coming from a shoot today. You chose your own wardrobe, right?

K: Yeah. You know, it's funny, the day before I left New York, I had a shoot for a big fashion magazine — kind of a gnarly, tortuous kind of scene that I hadn't experienced in a long time. The stylist kept trying to put me in modelly, overly designed things, and chiffon, and a beaded top with wraparound, with a leather vest over it. I was like, 'No, it's not happening.'

S: You have a lot of experience of the clothes business.

K: Well, I'm not doing that any more but what always interested me was cool things you'd want to wear. What's good to wear every day, like a cool shoe that's not too high. So I know about clothes. I don't know about *fashion*.

S: I think that's an important distinction.

K: I'm interested in advertising, in visuals. I like looking at ads, reading copy, seeing how things are packaged. But fashion people always seem so nerdy to me. It just seems like the opposite of style — it's rare when somebody cannot be nerdy in fashion.

8. CHRISTINE BARANSKI
—
Vanity Fair has named Diane Lockhart, the high-powered lawyer played by Christine Baranski, as one of the ten best-dressed characters on TV. Her immaculate suits are sourced from designers including Salvatore Ferragamo, Escada and Givenchy.

Kim Gordon was photographed in Echo Park, LA. It's a neighbourhood she knows well, having absconded to it during a recent winter to get away from the Massachusetts snow. Photography assistance: Ross Fraser. Make up: Roz Music. Production: Helena Martel Seward

S: It must be hard to keep perspective when the world becomes a filter for fashion.

K: There's so much out there, and yet it's hard to find anything wearable.

S: But that's true of so many things, in so many fields. The tyranny of choice doesn't make life easier; I think people are overwhelmed. Like, think about how the word *curator* is thrown around, how eager people are to have their choices narrowed down.

K: It's almost become an annoying word, because everyone's a curator.

S: But at the same time, it's cool that people have a certain flexibility. It seems right to me for example that you should be 'curating' that film night you're doing in New York, at the cinema at BAM, even though that's not technically your area of expertise.

K: I love film, and there are so many movies I love, but I wouldn't feel qualified to talk about film generally. So, it's clips and footage, music pieces I know well, things that have been important to me. I can choose this stuff but I worry about talking about it. Some people are so good at describing these things, like Jonathan Lethem. In *Dissident Gardens*, the way he captures the rehearsal process is the best description of being in a band I've ever read. I haven't read that much by him, but I *loved* that, and also *You Don't Love Me Yet*. I actually asked him to blurb my memoir, but he doesn't do that any more. I had a friend get in touch with him and he wrote back a really nice note, saying he was a big fan but that all these other writers would kill him. I also wanted Maggie Nelson — I love her essays — but my publisher didn't think she was a big enough name.

S: I've been meaning to read more by her. What's your favourite?
K: Probably *The Art of Cruelty*.

S: I'm making a note of it. Are there any other books that you think capture your experience the way Lethem did?
K: *The Flamethrowers* by Rachel Kushner — did you read it?

S: Yeah!
K: The way she describes the New York part, being a part of this world of older, established downtown artists — that was so vivid to me. And when I first read Warhol's *POPism* — the whole idea of Warhol, and the Factory — it was like somebody had handed me the keys to the city. Although, even then, his best stuff was behind him — and

all that stuff he did with Basquiat was so terrible. It really already felt like living history.

S: People talk a lot now about how New York is over. There's a sense that now there's no room to make art, or at least that no one can afford to.

K: I remember thinking that I'd already missed it because I wasn't around in the 70s. Thurston experienced all that: No Wave, Patti Smith, Television. But I didn't, and the 80s just felt like all the dregs left over. But there's a really good book, *Jack Goldstein and the CalArts Mafia*. He was an artist who was in between movements. He was included in the Pictures Generation, but he really came out of conceptual art. He ended up killing himself. The book is interviews with different people who were involved in the art world in the 80s, during that whole explosion. It was fascinating to me, because I thought it was just me; I thought I was the only one who was weirded out by what was going on. But they were all weirded out, by being suddenly successful, by the money, by all the coke. It really is a great window into that time in the art world.

S: Have you read either of Renata Adler's novels? *Speedboat* in particular seems to really capture 70s New York.

K: Oh, I'm writing that down. There are so many writers I want to read more of. Like, my daughter just read Lydia Davis and really loved it, so I want to read her.

S: You mentioned not feeling qualified to talk about certain art forms but it struck me that now most people don't feel that hesitation, in the age of the internet, of social media. You're on Twitter, aren't you?

K: Yes, and I started out mostly following comedians. Twitter's great for that, because they can distil material to that one perfect joke. It's probably great for trying material out. I started out trying to be funny, but people didn't really get my humour — it wasn't private, it was just open — so now I mostly just retweet things.

S: Were people nasty to you?

K: Once or twice, and then other people would jump in, and it would blow up into a whole thing. It's easy to see how people get into Twitter wars, how things go viral so fast.

S: Words like 'favourite' and 'like' are so loaded. Do you think you'll fall into reading Amazon reviews of your memoir? Do you read reviews, period?

9. THUNDERS
—
Johnny Thunders and David Johansen were key members of the New York Dolls, the extravagant New York punk band to precede all punk bands – they split up in 1975 just as punk started to happen. Johansen went solo and later reinvented himself as the somewhat slick singer Buster Poindexter. Thunders remained true to punk rock and toured tirelessly until his drug-fuelled death in 1991.

K: I always try to read reviews, unless I know they're really positive. And even then, I try to skim them. But I tend to get self-conscious, and I always feel like if things are really positive, it's almost putting a hex on you, jinxing you. And you have to be your own critic. But I've read some really mean things.

S: Are you good at taking criticism?

K: Not really. I've gotten a little better over the years.

S: I can imagine that it might be hard with such personal material, too.

K: Yeah. I did this interview yesterday, and he asked me something, and I just — it was just the mood I was in — I just started crying! I thought, oh God, this is going to be brutal, and it's just starting.

S: Did you ever get self-conscious writing the book? Imagining people reading about your private life, your family, your marriage?

K: Definitely. Strangely I worried most about getting facts right about music and stuff that may not be as important, but I didn't want the book to be discounted because of some factual error. I'd have to constantly second-guess my memory: oh, maybe it *wasn't* Johnny Thunders who sang that night! Maybe it was David Johansen! I went back and forth, and finally I asked a friend, who happened to have read an article where David Johansen talked about sometimes sitting in… anyway, that kind of thing really preoccupied me. I was careful. I knew that whatever I wrote about Lee or Steve would annoy them. It's hard to write about people who are alive. I thought about Patti Smith writing about Mapplethorpe. Of course people who knew him were still around when *Just Kids* came out, but it's not the same. You can be a lot freer after they've died. It was hard.

S: Did your daughter read it before it went to press?

K: I talked to her about it. She didn't want to read it. I mean, she *does* want to read it, but she said it was fine to write it, and she'd wait until it was totally done. I showed her the pictures I was using. I thought she'd care most about that. And I warned her, 'I'm probably not talking about you enough. *That* might annoy you!'

At this point the conversation turns to Gordon's break-up with Moore. She subsequently requests we do not reproduce this part of the interview due to it being too painful, personal and, potentially, too hurtful for Coco.

S: Did you consider concluding the memoir before the break-up, just to avoid dealing with it?

K: No, because I thought it was so much a part of the story, and where I am now. And, obviously, it's one of the reasons people are interested. I couldn't avoid it. That was actually the first thing I wrote. I was thinking of making it into a novel, doing something creative with it (*laughs*).

S: Was it cathartic?
K: Yeah, because when I went back and reread it, and worked on it — I did modify it a lot — it seemed, after a few years, much more pedestrian. This is so common. People lead double lives all the time, which is weird, but they do. Like that show *The Affair*. But I thought, even if it is something that happens all the time, the fact that it happened to me might be interesting. Well, to me, anyway.

S: In his *Paris Review* interview in 1986 the French author Alain Robbe-Grillet talks about how 'memory belongs to the imagination'.
K: The artist John Knight turned me on to Robbe-Grillet. I had never known writing could be like that, that you could write a novel like *The Voyeur*: how he builds up the mystery, and subtext. It seemed really filmic to me. I did some early work that was really influenced by it: little short stories and pieces, very noir and atmospheric, and repetitive.

S: I love what he does in that novel with ambiguity — it has one of the great unreliable narrators.
K: The voice is amazing.

S: Do you think you're especially drawn to the first person?
K: It's true. Didion, Mary Karr, and I love Mary Gaitskill's *Bad Behavior* too.

S: She's another one who you could say has a certain hard-edged quality to her prose that's not considered traditionally feminine, while focusing on the female sphere: women's relationships to each other, to the world...
K: The way she talks about female sexuality really stood out for me. I love what she wrote about the new passive guy, like meeting somebody at a party and having some kind of a flirtation, and you think you're going to go home together, even going so far as to walk out the door, and then having him walk away. The power dynamic is turned around.

S: In some way it makes me think of *I'm with the Band*, rock groupie Pamela Des Barres' fabulous memoir...

"Curator has almost become an annoying word, because everyone's a curator."

K: Right. Because bands have a lot of power, and she kind of seized it. She really did talk about that power dynamic, but then all relationships are about power dynamics. When I first read *I'm with the Band*, I found it really inspiring, in that: well, if she can write a book, I can. She didn't go to college or study writing. She just did it through sheer will and gumption. And it was really entertaining. I was struck by the fact that she's somebody who didn't feel like she had to achieve anything. Or, I don't know, maybe she did, and that's why she wrote the book. But it's so the opposite of me. I feel like I have to work and produce things in order to feel good about myself. And she's one of those people that really didn't! She felt good about sleeping with somebody who did something. And I know that sounds really regressive, but I think she had a great sense of self. Well, I don't know whether she had a horrible sense of self-worth or good sense of self-worth, but whatever it was, it was inspiring. It's really one of my favourite music books. And it's a point of view of the music world you don't often hear: a woman's point of view.

10. JAMES FREY

Media hell broke loose when it turned out that James Frey's 2003 book *A Million Little Pieces*, marketed as a memoir, was in fact riddled with fibs. In an awkward confession on *The Oprah Winfrey Show* ('I feel that you betrayed millions of readers'), pictured, he blamed 'demons'. Now re-listed under both 'memoir' and 'speculative fiction', it remains a strong seller.

S: And now you've contributed to that genre.

K: Years ago, when I wrote a tour diary for *Village Voice Rock and Roll Quarterly* — and it *was* a fake tour diary, because I'm not a journal-keeper — I got such a big response to it that I thought, maybe I could write a memoir, maybe I could do this. But in part, one of the reasons I did it was to make money. I need to open up other avenues of money. You know, I lost my main source of income when Sonic Youth split up. So I thought, well, if I'm going to do it, I can always make it interesting. And then I read Dylan's *Chronicles*, and I thought, I want to write a book where I just make stuff up, too! I originally wanted my memoir to be more arty and not as conventional.

S: Ten years ago everyone was so outraged by James Frey's largely fabricated memoirs, and now it feels like you could say, 'Oh, it's an unconventional metafiction', and everyone would be like, 'Oh, OK.'

K: Yeah, the fact that he posited it as memoir was such a problem for people.

S: And Oprah was taken in.

K: He could have just turned it around and said it was a conceptual art piece to play the game and see how the machine worked. He could have totally done that.

S: It would be harder to do, now the internet has come of age. We're so jaded about this idea of identity. We've arrived at this strange combination of a complete lack of privacy, combined, in some areas, with huge caution, legally speaking.

K: Right, that's true. What do you think about the whole — is there a line you step over, with comedy, with satire, like with the *Charlie Hebdo* cartoons?

S: I mean, in many ways that's an ideal example. Because the cartoons are not particularly witty or funny. It would be great if we were talking about *Ulysses*; if provocative things were thought-provoking rather than merely offensive, or a really stupid James Franco movie. But at the same time, that makes the principle so stark. That's free speech.

K: Mediocre art has to exist, too!

S: Speaking of which, did you watch *The Interview*?

K: It was horrible! I couldn't watch the whole thing. My friend watched it with her boys and she was like, 'It's not so bad.' But I think that's because she watched it with a twelve-year-old.

S: The *New York Times* critic watched it with his kid, too! Maybe that's the secret.

K: Exactly. Another movie I just watched is *Inherent Vice*.

S: Based on the Thomas Pynchon novel... Any good?

K: Almost unwatchable.

S: Really? How so?

K: I fell asleep. It had amazing parts and it looked amazing, but it was so... does the director smoke a lot of pot? What's the deal? It hardly held together. It was like Wes Anderson meets David Lynch, or something. A lot of it was commentary on noir movies in the stupidest way. It's incredible that any movie gets made, and then that they can be so bad. Although, I think I'm going to do music for James Franco's new movie, *Zeroville*, based on Steve Erickson's book. It has a kind of *O Lucky Man!* vibe to it, and they want some guitar noise. If you insist!

S: They want the caviar of guitar noise!

K: It's fun doing a soundtrack if they send you a scene and you send something back, and it's not didactic, like, OK, we need this style music from point 31 seconds — that's more tedious. I think for an editor it's more interesting if it's collaborative. And I've heard that James Franco is like that. Nick Cave worked with him and said it was a good experience. You know what movie I really regret not seeing? Godard's *Goodbye to Language*. It's such a brilliant idea, filming scenes from everyday life in 3D.

S: Do you like the 3D trend?

K: When it's used like that, in interesting ways, yes. Usually it's not. Do you like 3D?

S: I think the 3D trend is discriminatory for those of us who wear glasses. I just saw the latest *The Hobbit* and I had to sit perfectly still with the goggles kind of perched on top of my regular glasses.

K: Did you like the movie?

S: They stretched the novel into a trilogy, and it feels forced. It's no *Lord of the Rings*, which I loved.

K: Me too. Also, Viggo Mortensen's not in it! I never read *The Hobbit*. It was one of those books everyone was reading in high school, and so I was like, I'm not reading *that*.

S: Well, you were reading Nietzsche!

K: Exactly.

SADIE STEIN is a Manhattan-based writer, a contributing editor of *The Paris Review* and a former editor at Jezebel.com. As a teenager she saw Sonic Youth play live; it remains one of her favourite memories.

Gordon enjoys great literature but she's also hooked on TV shows such as *Friday Night Lights* and *Homeland*.

SPRING READS

Kim shares a telling and enthralling list of seven must-reads for the most optimistic season of all.

THE VOYEUR
Alain Robbe-Grillet
(1955)

The whodunnit has to be the frontrunner for fiction readers since the beginning of (literary) time. Our intellectual yearning to solve mysteries is unabating. But what happens when the basic facts — the name of the victim, say — change from one chapter to the next? When someone we know died in chapter one, reappears in later chapters, and not in flashback? Robbe-Grillet broke every murder mystery rule with *The Voyeur* — all the more reason to grow a moustache and grab your magnifying glass.

THE LIARS' CLUB
Mary Karr
(1995)

This is a memoir that strikes at the gut. A delicately fractured, grotesquely acerbic retelling of a childhood defined by abuse, alcoholism and mental illness. Many have tried and failed to match Karr's ability to infuse personal tragedy with real humour but few have succeeded in avoiding the pitfalls of sentimentality. Hoping, but not expecting, that her book would help pay the bills, Karr could not have anticipated she would set the standard of a genre.

THE KILLER INSIDE ME
Jim Thompson
(1952)

Long before Bret Easton Ellis gave us the hypnotic Patrick Bateman, Jim Thompson conjured up the original American psycho. Beneath his utterly regular façade there is a sadistic, sociopathic sickness that will plague even Christian Bale's biggest fan. R-rated entertainment.

NAUSEA
Jean-Paul Sartre
(1938)

    This is post-holiday blues to the extreme. The hero, Antoine, returns from his travels and becomes haunted by a 'sweet sickness' that seeps into every part of his life: his job, his relationships, his memory and even his own body. Try as he might, he cannot reconcile the failings of the physical world with his philosophical desires. Good old existentialism.

THE WHITE ALBUM
Joan Didion
(1979)

    Long before she was the face of international mega-brand Céline, Didion penned *The White Album* — a collection of essays that defined an era. Through her feminine, deeply introspective, partly hallucinogenic lens, the author brings 60s LA to life, in all its listlessness.

POPISM
Andy Warhol
(1980)

    At the centre of the cultural storm that seductively swept through 60s New York was the silver-haired Factory king, Andrew Warhola. Having dropped the 'a' from his surname, the artist simultaneously witnessed and fronted the avant-garde. In *POPism*, Warhol intimately reconstructs the era of Bob Dylan, Edie Sedgwick and the *Velvet Underground*, offering us the inside scoop from inside his den of innovation and decadence.

I'M WITH THE BAND
Pamela Des Barres
(1987)

    Pamela Des Barres is the ultimate star chaser, the 'sweetheart of rock'. She began by fantasising about Mick Jagger's balls in her high school art class and ended up on the road with the Stones. With honesty and warmth, she relays her time alongside some of the coolest musicians to have lived. Following her heart, she discovers a world of philosophy and psychology that educates her mind. She did for groupies what Miley Cyrus did for wrecking balls.

THE HAPPY
READER

Tea, a beverage loved everywhere from British caffs to the flanks of the Himalayan highlands, is both a central theme and a mere starting point to part two of The Happy Reader, steeped as it is in Kakuzo Okakura's THE BOOK OF TEA, a staggering work of libatory philosophy.

Bookish Quarterly — Issue nº 2

"Tea began as a medicine and grew into a beverage."

OPENING LINE
At first glance the sentence that begins *The Book of Tea* seems like a simple statement of fact. But then the reader will surely do a double-take and wonder: in what way is a beverage more evolved than a medicine? They are about to find out.

INTRODUCTION

As the afternoons regain the territory they lost to the dark winter evenings, it's the ideal time to read Kakuzo Okakura's extraordinary masterpiece, *The Book of Tea*, preferably with a cup of hot water poured over some favourite dried leaves. SEB EMINA introduces the second Book of the Season, a work filled, like spring ought to be, with tea, flowers, and wit.

HYPNOTISED BY A HOT DRINK

For those whose job or habit it is to arrange books into their proper categories, *The Book of Tea* is a bit of a problem. On which shelf does it belong? On the surface it is, as the title suggests, a book about tea, but to slot it into 'food and drink' won't work, because it's also at least as much about beauty, nature, religion, the relationship between East and West, the relationship between past and present, and how best to live one's life. It is also very funny, so neither 'philosophy' nor 'theology' will do, but 'humour' isn't the solution either, because Okakura is not here for laughs but rather uses his wit in the way of a statesman who knows a self-effacing manner is the best way of disarming a sceptical crowd. And then, so there is no doubting his underlying seriousness, *The Book of Tea* ends with a death.

A maverick librarian might argue for 'history', 'art', 'Japan studies', 'interior design' or 'floristry'. A wise bookshop will have a copy in every section, even 'motoring'. Cars are never mentioned (Okakura famously used to show up for work on a horse), but there is much in its ideas surrounding Zen that will be helpful to a learner driver. Failing that, 'classic literature' will do. Or, on second thought, perhaps 'food and drink' was fine after all, as Okakura is not one to pooh-pooh the importance of little things, least of all those we imbibe with ceremonial, daily regularity. When he addresses the history of the drink as it rose to prominence in China, Japan and the rest of the world, we are in the presence of some of the finest food writing ever committed to print. This book is about tea, it really is — but what is tea about? More than we might think, and so *The Book of Tea* is tricky to categorise.

Tea has been treated as medicine, poetry, commodity and much else besides. Like art, Okakura writes, tea has its classic, romantic and naturalistic schools. These take the form of three methods of preparation, which, in historic order, are: boiled, whipped and steeped. The last of these styles dominates twenty-first-century brewing, but the others are very much still in play. Matcha, the whipped tea used in the formal tea ceremony, is making inroads into western hot drink markets.

Having been educated at a Western-style school in Yokohama, Okakura was ideally placed to identify the common ground between societies who so often imagined that no common ground existed. Europeans and Americans may see the tea ceremony as an example of 'the quaintness and childishness of the East', he writes, but it works both ways: Japanese writers once said of Europeans that

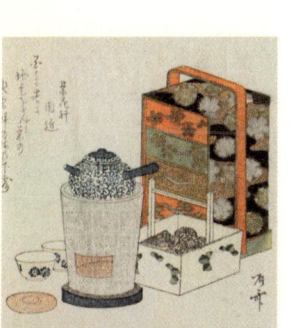
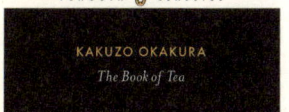

they had bushy tails hidden in their clothes. *The Book of Tea* tells us that while the tea ceremony is integral to Japanese culture, the values it represents are — or could be — universal. It is what happens when you take an element of everyday life, a cuppa, and treat it as seriously as you treat the highest forms of art. He calls this philosophy Teaism, and Teaism applies to us all: the first chapter of *The Book of Tea* is called 'The Cup of Humanity'.

It's a short book, an extended essay of seven chapters. You could read one chapter a day for a week. You could drink a cup of tea with each chapter, and it will take around the same time to read the chapter as it does to drink the cup. There ought to be a Teaism section in the bookshop so we finally know where to find *The Book of Tea*, though Okakura would likely have argued that all books, ultimately, belong there.

The philosophy of tea, declares Okakura, is to be taken seriously — so seriously it should be known as 'Teaism'. In Japan, this finds expression in the formal tea ceremony, but every tea-sipping nation has its own particular take. For example, writes NICHOLAS LEZARD, the British version of Teaism involves knowing there is a correct tea-making method, and disagreeing bitterly about what it is.

A SERIOUS CUPPA

I have just made a cup of tea. It is the right temperature — a little too hot to drink right now, but in a couple of sentences time it will have cooled down to just that degree when it becomes very hard to stop drinking it, and you feel that it could be delivered in the way a goose is fed to make foie gras — and, most importantly, it is the right taste. I know it is the right taste even though I have not sipped it yet because I have made it properly. I have made it in a pot, with leaves, and put the milk in the mug first (it is cold in the kitchen, and the mug was chilled, so I warmed it up with the boiling water I had already used to warm up the teapot; and if you think this is insane then you haven't seen nothing yet); and I was very careful about the temperature of the water and the milk I used. These things are important.

Britain is said to be the nation that cares about its tea more than all others, with the exception of Japan, and possibly China. And possibly India. Or Russia. Or... I know a young Iranian woman who is very particular about her tea. She goes miles out of her way to get it from a shop in Golders Green of all places, and making it involves what she was worried (she was busy in the kitchen and needed to teach me) would seem an enormous amount of faff; but no. While it was to me an alien technique, the principle of faff in making tea is itself very un-alien; and as it turned out this way of making tea, which I gather is rather similar to the way it is made in a Russian samovar, results in something approaching that which can be said to be the holy grail of tea drinkers: the pot which never runs out. You make it very strong, keep it on the hob, and dilute with freshly boiled water when you want a cup. It does run out in the end, of course, but a pot lasts all day, and the tea leaves themselves have this mysterious property: that they can be kept on the

---

1. SAMOVAR

A samovar is a rounded metal container used to heat and boil water in traditional Russian households. Nobody knows who invented the samovar but the first documented samovar-makers were two brothers, Ivan and Nazar Fyodorovich, who registered a samovar factory in 1778.

stove for hours without the tea itself stewing. I remember when London buses started using their more environmentally friendly engines, and realising that, weirdly, their exhaust fumes smelled almost exactly like stewed tea; the fact that I was able to identify the smell so quickly was a testament to experience: for it is only the British, I fear, who know the smell of stewed tea, being responsible for so much of it. For a nation which is said to be so hung up about its tea, it produces an awful lot of barely drinkable stuff.

It is the combination of utilitarianism, suspicion of the aesthetic, and bloody-mindedness that produces such a result. I have a friend who once, when I gently suggested he was not making the tea properly, said it was his own teapot, and he'd piss in it if he wanted to; laudable in his ferocious independence, but not the kind of statement that makes you feel like you want a cup of tea from him, just in case he has pissed in it. And yet he is far more English, by blood, than I am.

Faintly, though, the notion that tea has to be made in a certain way persists in these benighted islands. There is a civilisation to tea; the Japanese taught us this. (I once heard that when tea first started being imported to Britain in the seventeenth century, the infused leaves were spread on bread and butter, and the liquid was thrown away. I think I was being teased. What is beyond dispute, though, is that in the eighteenth century, the word 'tea' was pronounced 'tay'.) Theirs involves an incredible amount of faffing about. You have to make it in the right room, for instance, or have different types of tea for the seasons; there are many who insist on having appropriate hanging scrolls, with appropriate calligraphy expressing appropriate thoughts. This is before we even get to the appropriate clothing, flowers and food. In the United Kingdom — this is one of the few things that makes us a United Kingdom — the ideal food is a bacon sandwich, and the ideal clothing a dressing gown, which has at least the virtue of being roughly in the same shape and proportions as a kimono.

Exigencies of modern life have trimmed these rituals to the bone. In 1946, George Orwell wrote a short essay called 'A Nice Cup of Tea'

2. UTILITARIANISM

The skeleton of Jeremy Bentham, the founder of utilitarianism, is on permanent display in the main building of University College London; his bones padded with hay and dressed, with a wax head in place of his skull. As utilitarianism measures right and wrong based on the greatest happiness brought to the greatest number, Bentham would have delighted in UCL recently uploading a 360-degree rotatable version of what he called his "auto-icon" to the world wide web.

In cold climates, a tea cosy can be a welcome accessory.

THE HAPPY READER

THE BOOK OF TEA

BUILDER'S TEA
The British English for 'mug of black tea with milk, maybe sugar' is 'builder's', from its status as the preferred on-the-job beverage for those in the construction industry. COLIN DODGSON photographed a good example in a classic greasy spoon (also see p33) with a hearty baked-beans-based breakfast.

in which he laid down his eleven 'golden' rules for making tea — 'on perhaps two of them there would be pretty general agreement, but at least four others are acutely controversial.' Christopher Hitchens, his final days poisoned with exasperation at his inability to find a decent cup of tea in his adopted America, resurrected this essay in 2011, and although one agrees — OK, I agree — with ten of Orwell's points (at issue is whether one puts the milk in the cup first or not, to which the correct answer is milk goes in first, a point on which I am so self-evidently right that I am going to have to confine my reasons to a postscript), it becomes clear that what is important is not that everyone agrees, but that everyone disagrees. It is the acute controversy that we come for, as much as the tea. Except, of course, in my case. That Iranian woman I mentioned earlier? She loves the way I make my tea, to the point where I will be rebuked — in my own home! — if I have not followed my own rules strictly enough.

And yet I am in a vanishing minority in this country. Such ceremony as exists around the presentation of tea here revolves around the fact of communality and generosity rather than the taste of the stuff. The point is to offer a mug of hot, brown liquid, something soothing, not too caffeinated, into which you can dunk a biscuit, and, while sipping at it, go into a kind of reverie. The pause for tea is a fermata: a cessation of time, and worry. (You have coffee by your side when you're working, not tea. Coffee is horribly uncivilised like that. Remember how I began this piece, with a mug of tea by my side? I didn't write a word until I'd finished it. It would have been sacrilegious.) The tea-break is our way of approaching a state of nirvana — and I am being serious in my use of the word here: sitting with a cup of tea means the cessation of all desire, all dissatisfaction. You are bound only by the second law of thermodynamics, the gradual cooling of the tea. You have to start off with it very hot not only because that's how the leaves infuse, but because you want to take your time drinking it.

The problem lies in the modern age with the invention of the tea bag (or 'the humble tea bag', as it is routinely described by people unafraid of cliché). 'Nowadays it would be hard for many tea drinkers to imagine life without them,' says the UK Tea and Infusions Association, an assertion to which we can ruefully assent. Whether the tea bag is the cause, or the symptom, of the ills of contemporary society is hard to say. I'd say it can be either. 'When I makes tea I makes tea,' as Old Mother Grogan is reported as saying in *Ulysses*, 'and when I makes water, I makes water,' but the rise of the tea bag makes it only too easy to produce something piss-weak. In 2004, tea bags made 96% of our cups of tea; the figure can't have got any lower a decade hence, and it is almost a miracle that I can still find my Assam leaves in a supermarket. Tea bags, filled with the sweepings of the factory floor, allow the drinker to have her cup in miserable solitude; and the retailer to charge an outrageous mark-up for what is, in essence, a tiny sack of dust. I ask for two tea bags in my tea when I go to a cafe for my fry-up; this marks me out as a weirdo, but I am too old to give a damn. I recently asked for this in the Bridge Cafe on the High Street in West Hampstead, and was met with the baffled but polite rebuke that they did not, unless specifically requested, use tea bags; their tea came from a large pot, which might have broken Orwell's second rule ('Tea out of an urn is always tasteless,' etc.), but compared to tea-bag tea, a horror Orwell

4. RULES

Orwell's rules (or, as some have described them, preferences) in full:
i. Use only Indian or Ceylon tea.
ii. Make tea in a teapot (not in an urn or cauldron).
iii. Warm the teapot before use.
iv. Tea should be strong.
v. Loose tea leaves should be added to the pot – not put into baskets or strainers.
vi. The water should be boiling when added to the teapot, not just off the boil.
vii. Once the tea has infused, stir the pot and let the tea leaves settle.
viii. Pour the tea into a mug, not a teacup.
ix. Pour the cream off the milk before pouring milk into your tea (this one doesn't really apply anymore).
x. Tea first, milk second.
xi. No sugar.

5. CHRISTOPHER HITCHENS

The author Christopher Hitchens (1949–2011) resided at 2022 Columbia Road in northwest Washington DC in an apartment building named The Wyoming. His real-estate choice placed him only three blocks away from Michelle Brown and Linda Neumann's specialist tea shop called Teaism, which has four locations throughout the city.

AUTHOR
Kakuzo Okakura (1862–1913), portrayed by CLYM EVERNDEN. The Yokohama-born scholar would arrive at Tokyo Fine Arts School, of which he was director, dressed in a white robe, and mounted on a white stallion. Avid readers of his work included the British-American poet TS Eliot, the Indian monk Swami Vivekananda and the German philosopher Martin Heidegger.

was spared, the Bridge Cafe's tea was like manna, and I thoroughly endorse this most splendid institution. Otherwise, the sheer fucking cheek of charging north of two quid for some not-quite-hot-enough water and a tea bag costing around ten pence at the very most, is nothing more than a bald illustration of the way that capitalism, taken beyond a certain point, can demonstrate its contempt for the ordinary citizen. And now we know the exact proportion of society which resists the pressure of utility, which still thinks it worth spending two extra minutes to produce something more comforting and tasty than just a hot, brown liquid: 4%. Four. I hope it's enough.

POSTSCRIPT — The reason Orwell said the milk should go in after the tea is because if one doesn't do this, one never quite knows until it is too late whether one has put in enough, too little, or too much milk. To which one might reply: if, after drinking countless thousands of cups of tea, one is unable to judge how much milk one has to put in the bottom of the cup, one has no business in the kitchen at all. As far as the contemporary debate goes, we live in such debased times that the question of milk in first/second now presupposes a world in which the teapot is a distant memory, and tea now is only made monadically, in a mug. And when I first heard that there were people who were capable of putting in the milk, then the tea bag, THEN the hot water, I thought to myself: it's over. The whole Enlightenment project. Ashes and dust.

NICHOLAS LEZARD writes about books for *The Guardian*, and about himself for *The New Statesman*. He lives in London, and guards his teapot with fierce and unwavering dedication.

AROUND TOWN

Today, few places have a more inspiring relationship with flowers than Paris, where overgrown floristry shops contribute so much to the city's living beauty and social etiquettes. THOMAS CHATTERTON WILLIAMS visits Muse, a precise florist with an extraordinary following.

THE EXACTITUDE OF A BOUQUET

In 2010 the acclaimed designer and reputedly formidable amateur horticulturist John Galliano, then at Dior, showed a remarkable autumn couture collection seemingly fabricated by Mother Nature herself. Stem-limbed models strutted down the catwalk in colourful swathes of fabric ruffled and fluted to look like flower petals in shifting sunlight, their heads encased in cellophane. If the inspiration behind this presentation wasn't already apparent, by the time the editors and critics in attendance returned to their hotel suites around Paris, the overflowing bouquets wrapped in plastic and cinched with cords of raffia that were waiting for them would certainly drive the point home.

The man responsible for these wondrous arrangements, as well as the supplier of Galliano's practically insatiable personal floral habit, is a softly spoken 42-year-old Iranian with a meticulously trimmed

A deliriously joyful bouquet concocted by Majid Mohammad for this very page of *The Happy Reader*, as photographed in his shop in Paris by Damian Noszkowicz.

moustache and gentle bearing named Majid Mohammad. An accountant by training, he fell into his life's vocation by accident nearly two decades ago in Tehran. 'Basically, I got fired and wasn't working,' Mohammad, dressed in a knitted beanie and blue jeans cuffed loosely over polychromatic Air Maxes, explains from behind the small counter at Muse, his exquisite, black-painted boutique on the rue Burq, at the base of Montmartre. 'By chance, a surgeon friend who owned two flower shops for the fun of it asked me to help out. It pleased me, so I stayed.'

In the years since that fateful request, Mohammad has hit upon and refined a style that distinguishes his work in Paris's competitive if staid flower industry. Composing a bouquet, he explains, 'depends on the person the flowers will be given to, whether it's a woman or a man, and on the occasion'. And it should also depend on the season. The vessel used to hold the flowers becomes a crucial point of consideration, as does something so subtle as the water level inside the vase. 'That's important too,' he stresses, 'but it's not always so obvious at the moment you start to mix together different vegetation.' Finally, Mohammad always looks to 'unite flowers that are architecturally similar', regardless of colour. This can lead to some counter-intuitive combinations, such as the exploding sphere of colour he is presently building around waxflower and a grassy bunch of *oeillets japonais*.

After he moved with his family to Paris in 2000 — and without speaking any French — such innate aesthetic sense allowed Mohammad to quickly assume the role of director of l'Artisan Fleuriste, an institution with a smart clientele on the rue Vieille du Temple, in the upper Marais. It was there that his work caught the discerning eye of Galliano, a neighbourhood fixture (whose temporary fall from fashion grace, one may recall, sprang from anti-Semitic remarks made at a cafe table down the street) and a man who buys fresh flowers with a passion bordering on mania. 'This is somebody who is very accurate, especially about flowers,' Mohammad explains. 'He doesn't like just anything.'

6. RUE BURQ

Prior to 1863, the Rue Burq existed as a dirt lane named Chemin des Behourdes, after an Old French word for the lance used during a tournament between knights.

7. WAXFLOWER

The naturally occurring waxflower plant, genus *Chamelaucium*, should not be confused with the fake flower variety, although it was discovered shortly before the great wax flower craze of Victorian England. It is said that Queen Victoria adored wax flowers and had 10,000 white roses molded from wax when she married her beloved Albert.

Which is why, since 2009, at least once a week, Mohammad has personally sourced, prepared and delivered complicated and sometimes colour-specific bouquets for every single room of Galliano's apartment. 'He's a very important client for me,' he admits, 'my biggest, in fact, since the large bouquets start at 150 euros.' This is to say nothing of the additional orders the designer, who recently took over Maison Martin Margiela, requires in all of his offices and workspaces.

Along with Pierre Debeaulieu in the ninth arrondissement and a handful of other voguish young florists around town, Mohammad is not unaccustomed to the world of high fashion and the demand that exists there for his specific expertise. At l'Artisan Fleuriste, he often supplied designers Kris Van Assche, Phillip Lim and Ann Demeulemeester. But when it comes to working with design studios and showrooms, the reality is that the chicest clients usually ask for the plainest, all-white arrangements, which Mohammad finds boring. 'Personally, I love bouquets that are wild, that's my taste. Or sometimes, I really like just one type of flower, such as roses, but mixed by size — this is beautiful,' he gushes. 'I love that unexpected thing, to make very wild bouquets, mystical and vaporous combinations in the spirit of a magic garden.'

Like every other florist in Paris, Mohammad must rise several times a week at three in the morning to scour the sprawling, centuries-old wholesale market that moved in the 1960s from Les Halles to the suburb of Rungis, where the flower business alone represents 186 million euros annually. 'Everyone goes there,' he shrugs. 'Unfortunately, in the winter there's not much choice, but I try to stand out by focusing on what's in season.' He supplements his selection with exotic varieties — some that are new, and some that are all but forgotten or deemed passé, such as carnations, gladiolas, tuberoses and celosia. 'Exotic flowers don't please everyone,' he admits, but there are some beautiful varieties, as the livid red cluster of kangaroo paw leaning against the wall can attest.

Another signature flourish of Mohammad's is to sheath special bouquets in vintage sheet music, like Puccini's *Tosca*, that he keeps in stacks beneath the counter. It's a nice touch, and goes well with the classical melodies playing in the background at Muse. He smiles at the mention of a link between flowers and art, specifically literature, acknowledging that he tries to arrange his store like a poem. And there is indeed something poetic about the whole operation when one considers the history of floral symbolism throughout the Romantic tradition, stretching all the way back to Goethe's vain quest for the *Urpflanze* in Italy.

But just when things threaten to get too highfalutin, Mohammad brings the conversation back down to earth. 'My mother is a hairdresser, you know, but very creative, too. She's always been crazy about flowers. When I was little, she would always put flowers in my room, sometimes just a single flower, but she would do it every day.' And now, he says, his face brightening, the roles have reversed: 'Now, every week when I see her, I have to take her several bouquets, too.' And with that, Majid cinches up the the *oeillets japonais* he's been perfecting until now, handing off the arrangement to the delivery man waiting by the door — a whimsical radiance released into the grey Parisian street.

8. ANN DEMEULE-MEESTER

Belgian designer Ann Demeulemeester lives in Antwerp, Belgium, but the eponymous label that she founded in 1985 presents its collections during fashion week in Paris. These days Ann herself has no direct need to be in Paris anymore since she announced her departure from the brand in 2013. Her last act in the field of fashion came in the form of a retrospective book that was published in October 2014 and contained a whopping 2028 pages.

9. QUEST

The southern leg of Goethe's famous Italian Journey was partially dedicated to the search for the *Urpflanze*, a plant species that he believed would be the genetic archetype of all plants.

A few years ago, THOMAS CHATTERTON WILLIAMS wrote a memoir called *Losing My Cool: Love, Literature and a Black Man's Escape from the Crowd*. These days he's living in Pigalle, Paris.

MANUAL

It's easy to cobble together a passable cup of tea, but to make one that transports you, as the poet Lotung once whispered, 'to the realm of the immortals', will take precision, practise and freshly drawn water. Tea maestro JEFF KOEHLER has sought out perfect techniques for humanity's most popular brews, and is keen to share them.

PERFECT TEAS

There are six main classifications of tea — black, oolong, green, yellow, white and pu-erh — but they all come from the same plant, *camelia sinensis*. Tea's multitude of styles, shapes and grades is thanks to the way in which the leaves, once plucked, are processed. Equally, from any given kind of tea can be made a great variety of hot drinks, each correctly describable as a 'cup of tea': water temperature, leaf quantities and steeping times depend on the type of tea; no universal rule covers them all. The eight classic recipes that follow, then, can be seen as starting points rather than destinations. Taste and then adjust.

1. DRAGON WELL
(This method will work for all green teas)

Among the green teas of China, the most famous and arguably the most delicious is Dragon Well (*long jing*), grown on the hillsides of Hanghzou in Zhejiang Province. The flattened, folded yellowish-green leaves brew an exquisite liquor, smooth and fresh, with subtle hints of sweetness.

A pot for two:
 4tsp dragon well or other green tea
 Freshly drawn or bottled water

Rinse out a teapot with hot water to warm. Spoon in the tea. Bring a kettle of water to the boil then let cool for three minutes (perfect temperature: 75–82°C). Pour 350ml water over the leaves. Cover and steep for 2–3 min. Strain into cups.

2. SILVER NEEDLES
(This method will work for all white teas)

The finest, most delicate white tea is Silver Needles from the northern part of Fujian Province. Sword-shaped buds yield a silvery, champagne-coloured liquor, fresh and delicate in the mouth.

A pot for two:
 4tsp Silver Needles or other white tea
 Freshly drawn or bottled water

Rinse out a teapot with hot water to warm. Spoon in the tea. Bring a kettle of water to the boil then let cool for five minutes (perfect temperature: 75°C). Pour 350ml water over the leaves. Cover and steep for 2 min. Strain the tea into cups, preferably white or clear glass.

3. SECOND FLUSH DARJEELING

The champagne of teas, grown in the Indian Himalayas. Darjeeling sells by single estate like wines, and also by harvest season known as 'flush'. From mid-March to mid-November, shoots are plucked every week or so as they gradually move through first flush, second flush, monsoon flush and then finally autumn flush.
 While first flush has spring freshness, second flush is where Darjeeling's muscatel flavour is most pronounced. The liquor shines a brilliant copper. Best drunk without milk, sugar, or lemon.

THE HAPPY READER

1. DRAGON WELL

2. SILVER NEEDLES

5. HIMALAYAN BUTTER TEA

6. RUSSIAN TEA

The first sip is with the eye: the colours of tea in all their wondrous subtlety, perfectly made and photographed by MARIUS W. HANSEN

3. SECOND FLUSH DARJEELING

4. PU-ERH

7. KAHWA

8. MOROCCAN MINT

A pot for two:
    4 tsp second flush Darjeeling or other
        Darjeeling tea
    Freshly drawn or bottled water

Rinse out a teapot with hot water to warm. Spoon in the tea. Bring a kettle of water to the boil then let cool for one minute (perfect temperature: 88°C). Pour 350ml water over the leaves. Cover and steep for 3 min. Strain into cups, preferably white.

4. PU-ERH

From Yunnan in southwestern China. The dried tea is lightly steamed, pressed into cakes and aged in a darkened environment, often for years. Pieces are pried off using a blunt pu-erh pick. The leaves are often steeped several times: the strength, but also the astringency, dissipates, the earthy, woodsy flavours evolving slightly with each cup.

For a medium teapot:
    2 tbsp pu-erh tea
    Freshly drawn or bottled water

Pry flakes of tea from their cake by working a pu-erh pick or knife into it. Place in a small tea pot, preferably unglazed. Boil the kettle. Rinse the leaves by pouring in a little of the water and immediately pouring off. Now pour 300ml water over the leaves, cover and steep for between 20 seconds and 1 min. Strain into small tea cups. You can steep again when these are drunk. Each steeping should progressively increase in time slightly, depending on desired strength.

5. HIMALAYAN BUTTER TEA

Tea arrived in Tibet from eastern China along what was known as the Tea Horse Trail. Tibetans pounded the tea, soaked it in cool water, and then boiled it at length before churning the concentrate with yak butter, and often yak milk and salt. *Po cha* remains popular, although the dairy is often from cows and electric blenders have largely replaced tea churns.

For two bowls:
    Freshly drawn or bottled water
    1 tbsp loose Assam or Ceylon black tea or
        a robust unscented black tea blend that
        includes pu-erh
    60ml whole milk
    1 tbsp unsalted butter
    Salt

In a large saucepan, boil 420ml water then remove from the heat, add the tea, cover, and let steep for 5 min. Strain into a teapot and leave for 3–4 min. Now transfer the liquid to a blender and add the milk, butter and three pinches of salt. Blend until frothy. Now pour back into the saucepan, and return to a boil over medium-low heat. Serve scalding hot in tea bowls or large, sturdy glasses.

6. RUSSIAN TEA

Russia began importing tea from China in around the seventeenth century. The tea aged on the journey: it was 5,000 miles to Moscow, and by camel a round trip took sixteen months. Making Russian-style tea is a two-step process. A pot of concentrated tea, kept warm on top of a samovar, is diluted with hot water from the urn. It is sweetened with sugar, honey or a spoonful of jam — rose petal and strawberry are favourites — often dolloped into the cup before pouring in the tea. Here's a method for those without a samovar to hand.

A pot for four:
    Freshly drawn or bottled water
    2 tbsp black tea blend with around 25%
        lapsang souchong
    Rose petal, strawberry or another
        fruit jam
    Sugar
    Honey
    Lemon wedges

Bring a large kettle of water to a boil. Rinse a teapot with some of the water to warm. Spoon in the tea, cover the pot and leave for 1 min to soften in the residual steam. Pour in 240ml water, cover and steep for 5 min. Warm another teapot. Strain the tea from the first pot into that one. Dollop some jam (if desired) into four cups or Russian tea glasses. Into each cup or glass, pour some concentrated tea then dilute with at least the same amount again of boiled water, perhaps more: the final colour should be a rich chestnut or mahogany. Serve with jam, sugar, honey and lemon.

7. KAHWA

A Kashmiri end-of-meal drink with the brilliant yellow tone of a polished wedding ring. The green tea of choice is gunpowder, which comes in tightly rolled pellets that unfurl in the pot. If the gunpowder pellets are 'dusty' give them a very quick rinse with boiling water before steeping. Chopped almonds on top add earthy sweetness.

For two cups:
- 2 cardamom pods
- 1 clove
- 1.25cm piece cinnamon stick
- 1 small pinch saffron threads (8–12 threads)
- Freshly drawn or bottled water
- 2 tsp sugar
- 1 scant tbsp gunpowder green tea
- 5 skinless raw almonds, chopped

Crush the cardamom pods between thumb and forefinger. Add to a large saucepan with the clove, cinnamon and saffron. Pour in 480ml water and bring to a boil. Reduce the heat to low and simmer for 5 min. Remove from heat, add sugar and stir until dissolved. Meanwhile, rinse out a teapot with hot water to warm and spoon in the tea. Pour the spice-infused liquid over the tea leaves. Cover and leave for 5 min. Strain into two tea cups, preferably white porcelain. Scatter some almonds into each and serve.

8. MOROCCAN MINT

When tea arrived in North African ports in the mid nineteenth century, Moroccans rapidly embraced it. The national brew they devised did not involve milk or spices, but sugar and fistfuls of fresh herbs — mint, most famously, but others too. When Moroccan mint tea is poured from up high into tiny, ornate glasses, this is not just for dramatic effect. It re-aerates the water and the cascading sound announces that the tea is ready and requires guests' attention.

For two glasses:
- 1 scant tbsp gunpowder green tea (quickly rinse with boiling water if 'dusty')
- Freshly drawn or bottled water
- 3 tbsp sugar
- 1 small bunch fresh mint, rinsed and shaken dry, or a blend of mint with other fresh herbs such as marjoram, sage or absinthe (wormwood) leaves

In a stove-top teapot or saucepan, sprinkle in the tea. Cover with 400ml water and bring to a boil then turn the heat to low. Stir in the sugar. Gently stuff the mint leaves into the pot. Using the back of a large spoon, slightly crush some of the mint against the bottom of the pot. Simmer for 5 min. Begin blending the flavours by pouring off a glass and adding back into the pot. The liquor should cloud and turn amber. Taste for strength, sweetness and mintiness, letting it simmer as needed or adding more sugar. Continue to pour the tea back and forth with a glass and tasting until it's as desired. Arrange two small tea glasses on a tray. Pour the tea into them from as high as possible and serve scalding hot.

American writer JEFF KOEHLER'S latest book, *Darjeeling*, is essential reading for anyone with a newfound (or indeed oldfound) taste for tea history. A resident of Barcelona, Jeff's a regular at Čaj Chai, a bohemian teahouse in the Gothic Quarter.

ADDENDUM

"Nobody ever said: I'll make you a horrible cup of tea. It was always: I'll make you a nice cup of tea." — Morrissey, who travels with a favourite teapot and whose preferred brew is a very weak Ceylon.

HABITUAL LAYOUTS

A formal tea ceremony takes place in a tea room, or *sukiya*, a strictly defined space in which every element is carefully chosen and placed. While the host enters through a *sadouguchi*, a full-sized door, guests will come in on their hands and knees by way of a *nijiriguchi*, a small opening for crawling through. All will remove shoes or sandals before entering. The floor of a tea room is covered with *tatami* mats, one of which is a *temeaza*, a mat used by the tea master when making tea or lighting the charcoal fire. Inside an alcove called a *tokonoma* are displayed a *kakejiku* and a *chabana*, respectively a hanging scroll and an arrangement of flowers.

YOJOHAN
The *yojohan* is, in Okakura's words, the 'orthodox tea room': four-and-a-half mats in size, with the host sat in the middle. It is said to be the same size as the hut in which Yuima, a Buddhist saint from India, accommodated eighty-four thousand Buddhist disciples: 'an allegory,' observes *The Book of Tea*, 'based on the theory of the non-existence of space to the truly enlightened.'

A TATAMI AND A TEMEAZA
A small tea-room with just one guest mat plus a three-quarter size mat for the host. A hearth is built into the frontier between the host's mat and the guest's. A tea ceremony will only use this sunken hearth in autumn and winter; in spring and summer tea is made by way of a portable brazier, the hearth covered by a *tatami* mat. NB if being entirely traditional, the start of spring is defined as the moment when red buds are seen on a certain kind of shrub — the *kanamemochi*, or Chinese hawthorn.

DEEP THREE-MAT ROOM
A trio of mats, with a hearth between host and guests. The dimensions of a *tatami* vary according to region: the average is three feet by six feet. A traditional *tatami* is made from closely woven rush reeds, with a filling of straw and borders of cloth. When new, this kind of *tatami* is pale green, and it smells wonderful. As it ages, it turns yellow. The smell becomes less wonderful.

LONG FOUR-MAT ROOM
A somewhat informal but very ancient layout style. A host's mat might incorporate a utensil stand called a *daisu* holding items including whisks, cloths, scoops, ladles, water jars and ash containers. There is a strict choreography to these utensils, with principles in place that guide everything from the order in which they are displayed to the very hand in which they are carried.

LONG FOUR-MAT VARIATION
Slight differences in *tatami* layout can create significant changes in the atmosphere of a tea room. Each will come with its own long history, often stretching back for centuries.

MANIA

Tea, flowers, Zen and jiu jitsu: *The Book of Tea* contained much to fuel the West's infatuation with Japanese culture. ROLAND KELTS, an expert in western Japanophilia, identifies some of its more intriguing paradoxes.

WE LOVE JAPAN

'After living in Japan for a month, you'll want to write a novel. After a year, an article or three. Any longer than that, you'll write nothing at all.'

A Japanese friend told me this at a bar in Osaka one night. I didn't fully grasp the meaning of my friend's aphoristic saying at the time, but it made me laugh. It also made me want to write faster.

I had just moved to Osaka, having been commissioned to write a novella for an American magazine and film studio. I had visited many times as a child and teenager, traveling with my Japanese mother from the United States to see family, and once, to live with my grandparents and attend a local kindergarten. Essentially, I was being paid to understand enough of Japan to create and publish a story about the place.

The broader meaning of my friend's comment — the more you learn, the less you know — could be applied to nearly any subject of study or observation: familiarity can breed mystification as easily as contempt. But for Westerners, Japan has long been a peculiar case, a land many have found and continue to find both puzzling and irresistible, the tantalising jewel-in-the-crown of Orientalism, or 'the eternal east' both ancient and futuristic, and forever inscrutable.

That was in 1999, and I've lived in Japan ever since. But as I travel so frequently to the US and other parts of the world, I have cultivated a kind of double vision, an awareness of two Japans — one seen from within, the other from without — from which I probably both suffer and benefit. For me, the history of the West's bouts of 'Japanophilia' is very much about the Japan the Japanese want you to see. And that Japan, more than any other national character I know, is very well constructed.

The image presented to the outside world is less the product of deliberate fabrication (aside from the obvious tourism campaigns) and more the result of a way of seeing the world that is embedded in Japanese culture. In Japan, you don't just say what you feel; you say what you're supposed to say only when you're supposed to say it. Change the situation, the setting, the time of day, and the rules are suddenly different. Enter someone's home, take off your shoes. Enter the toilet room, don a separate pair of slippers. The strict demarcation of the external and the internal is expressed conceptually in binary terms like *uchi-soto* (inner vs. outer) and *honne-tatemae* (inner feelings vs. outer behaviour). Context is everything.

'The whole of Japan is a pure invention,' wrote the ultimate self-invented dandy, Oscar Wilde, in 1889. 'There is no such country, there are no such people.'

10. MATTHEW PERRY
—
A rather different figure to his *Friends* alumnus namesake, this renowned seaman recently gave his name to a US Navy dry cargo ship, 'the USNS Matthew Perry'.

11. VAN GOGH
—
'In a way,' mulled the painter in a letter to his brother Theo, 'all my work is founded on Japanese art.' He called this influence *Japonaiserie*. This was 1888. He died two years later, shortly after completing the celebrated *Portrait of Dr. Gachet*, which, a century later, sold at auction for a record $82.5m, having been bought by a Japanese collector. This collector was then arrested for bribery relating to a golf club he wanted to start — to be named 'Vincent'.

Wilde was writing at the peak of the first wave of Japanophilia in Europe, after a long self-isolated Japan had been pried open to international trade by an American naval fleet — Commodore Matthew Perry's so-called 'black ships' — a little over 30 years earlier. The attraction to all things apparently Japanese, then called *Japonisme*, was largely the province of the cognoscenti and the upper classes. Kimonoed geisha and white-faced kabuki players, cherry blossoms, Japanese fans and Mount Fuji all cropped up in works by van Gogh, Gauguin and Degas.

Most of the Japanese imagery that had been delivered to nineteenth-century Europeans had come courtesy of *ukiyo-e*, or woodblock prints, which were often used as wrapping paper for Japanese ceramics, vases, teapots and assorted bric-a-brac. The irony is rich and telling: the Japanese take great pride in the practice of *monozukuri* — roughly translated as making physical things exceptionally well. Yet it was the imagery used to wrap those things, the presentation of a Japan, that most fuelled European Japanophilia. That imagery, abstract, colourful line-based portraits of moments in 'the floating world' — transient pleasure quarters — celebrated the fundamentals of *wabi sabi*, the beauty of the imperfect, impermanent and incomplete.

Katsushika Hokusai, creator of the most recognisable and mass-produced woodblock print, *The Great Wave off Kanagawa*, also worked in a visual style that would become essential to Japanophilia: manga, or 'random sketches'. Manga focused on lower subjects — everyday life in Japan, street scenes and chance encounters — but they could also be erotic and comical. They were not exactly the graphic novels and comics that the term brings to mind today, but they were equally unrestricted in tone and material. (Fart jokes, for example, are not uncommon.)

Western Japanophiles have always been confronted with this kind of paradox. On the one hand: a Japan that is poetical, exquisitely crafted and sensitive to the subtlest qualities of human existence. On the other: an irreverent Japan that cracks open Pandora's Box, shamelessly, even smirking.

This view of Japan as a land of paradox is nothing new today, and it wasn't really in the nineteenth century. The first Westerners in Japan, at the time the farthest east of the Far Eastern lands, were Portuguese

Around it goes: Japanese pressing of a record by Japan, the English Japanophile new wave group who released nine UK top 40 singles in the early 1980s.

Jesuit missionaries in the mid-sixteenth century. They were spectacularly unsuccessful at converting the locals, and are most memorable now for having introduced a fish-frying method for lent that would become one of Japan's trademark cuisines: tempura. Then came the Dutch. Both kinds of intruder were relegated to the geographical margins of Japan, to islands off Nagasaki in the far south. They were seen as hairy, long-nosed barbarians to be banished or decapitated by feudal lords if seen as posing any kind of threat.

The foreigners returned the favour. They saw Japan as an antipodean wonder, a 'world the reverse of Europe,' backwards and upside down, a paradox within a riddle wrapped in endless kimono folds. Westerners were tall, Japanese short. Churches high, temples low. Western women had white teeth, Japanese blackened theirs. Western books opened left-to right, their languages streamed horizontally across the page; Japanese turned right-to-left, read top-to-bottom.

'On the one hand, the Japanese were commented upon for possessing a highly sophisticated, even over-refined, system of etiquette, by which every aspect of their conduct towards one another appeared to be determined,' writes Yoko Kawaguchi in *Butterfly's Sisters*, her 2010 study of Western encounters with Japanese women. 'It had, on the other hand, become a commonplace since the sixteenth century to charge the Japanese with lewdness.'

To win over the United States, Japan sent performing clowns and ambassadors of elegance. In the 1860s, an all-Japanese circus act (promoted by an enterprising American known as 'Professor Risley') dazzled audiences with acrobatic stunts featuring traditional Japanese fans, umbrellas and freakish contortions. In 1871, the Japanese government sent a quintet of noblewomen, daughters of samurai lineage, to San Francisco to learn American ways, and impress upon their hosts the sophistication of Japanese femininity. The girls were a hit. The thirst for Japanese culture grew and grew.

The next wave of Western Japanophilia spiked in the late 1950s and early 60s in the bohemian enclaves of postwar America. Beatniks and bohemians both sympathised with Japan's 'victimization' narrative in the wake of Hiroshima and Nagasaki, and found the pristine aesthetics and cool exteriors of that Far Eastern outpost sexy and pragmatic. In retrospect, the hand-wringing over Yoko Ono's supposed destruction of The Beatles via her marriage to John Lennon seems an acknowledgement of Japan's cultural power: Madama Butterfly is here to stay.

In the 1980s, Japan was an economic threat to the United States, so much so that anti-Japan bumper stickers were brandished in Middle America like anti-Arab rhetoric today. Slogans like 'I only buy American' appeared beside the American flag and hunched-over stick figures, or a red dot (Japan's rising sun flag) inside a circle with a diagonal line through it. (During a teaching stint at Princeton in the 80s, novelist Haruki Murakami, noting that the rising sun was so tiny, first thought the image meant, 'No umeboshi,' the small red pickled plumb at the centre of many Japanese rice dishes.) The Japanese were depicted as soulless labourers, impoverished automatons auguring a robotic Asian future. Few cultural institutions braved Japanese art exhibitions. Japan was envisioned as an industrial giant, but a cultural midget.

When the third wave hit in the 1990s, it was both different and familiar. Anime, manga and pop iconography, in the forms of Pokémon,

12. POKÉMON

Pokémon, which is currently a 24 billion dollar franchise, was inspired by insect collecting — a hobby common among Japanese kids. The anime became so popular that in 2001 the South Pacific island of Niue produced a run of one dollar coins with Pikachu on the back. The 'Electric Soldier Polygon' episode of the anime gained the Guinness World Record for 'Most Photosensitive Epileptic Seizures Caused By A TV Show', after almost 750 children in Japan were taken to hospital after viewing it on 16 December 1997.

Hello Kitty, and other arguably lightweight but Zeitgeist-slick graphics entranced the West with the same old contrasts — Japan is funny and light, but also intimate. Japan is peaceful, but playful, and sometimes demanding. Japan is rich and poor, smart and stupid, clever by half, and definitely not Chinese.

And how about those long-nosed barbarians? Well, the biggest story in the Japanese TV industry at the moment is about the first ever leading role performed by a non-Japanese actor. In a popular morning drama, Charlotte Kate Fox, an American, portrays Scotswoman Rita Cowan, who married Masataka Taketsuru, the founder of Nikka Whiskey, and moved to Japan in the 1920s. The media here is obsessed with the blond-haired, blue-eyed Fox. It's revealing: even after centuries of interloping and economic intertwinement, both Japan and the West still consider each other's culture, and people, as a tumble through a looking glass.

Japanophilia is unique inasmuch as Japan remains the sexiest other for the West. China — forget it. Too belligerent, and too much like us. And for Americans, Europe is too mired in the glories of Europe, while for Europeans, America is as tired as its presidents, black or white. But Japan remains an innocuous icon of honest fun. And it is. I live here, and I can tell you that Japan's achievements — no guns, clean streets, historical amnesia — keep the image of Japan, however artful and clever, buttressed by an admirably civilised reality. It may be well wrapped, but it's also well made.

ROLAND KELTS is the half-Japanese American author of *Japanamerica: How Japanese pop culture has invaded the US*. A contributing writer for *The New Yorker* and a columnist for *The Japan Times*, he divides his time between New York and Tokyo.

INTERLUDE

Before becoming a writer, NOEL 'RAZOR' SMITH spent a long time in prison. There are few places, he explains, where the tea is of worse quality — and fewer still where it is taken more seriously.

IN PRISON

When notorious prisoner Charles Bronson, once dubbed the 'most dangerous man in the British prison system', broke away from his escort and clambered onto the roof of Broadmoor Special Hospital in 1983 (the first of his three visits to the roof during his stay there) the first thing he requested was 'a nice cup of tea'. Fortified by his tea he set to work on ripping the entire roof from Kent Wing, causing hundreds of thousands of pounds' worth of damage. Charlie, like the majority of prisoners, dangerous or otherwise, does love a cup of Rosie Lee.

I have always been a big tea drinker, and three decades of drinking prison tea has done nothing to blunt my enthusiasm for this refreshing amber beverage. Tea is very popular in the British prison system, though the tea that is supplied to the inmates would not be a taste that those in the free world would choose or recognise. Traditionally prison tea is made in huge urns, or 'coppers', which are the size of a skip, and stirred with a paddle that would not be out of place on a lifeboat. The copper is filled with fifty gallons of water and then a muslin bag containing loose, but very poor quality, tea leaves, weighing around fifteen pounds, is lowered into the water and left to boil, sometimes for twelve hours. The Prison Service catering departments are mindful of reducing costs and balancing their budgets and so purchase the absolute cheapest products, including tea.

Prison tea is universally known as 'diesel' by prison inmates, and this is due not only to the bitter taste but also to the fact that it invariably has a 'rainbow' effect on its surface, rather like spilled diesel fuel on a wet road. Milk is added to the coppers once the water has boiled so as to lighten the colour of the brew. But, ever mindful of the tightness of prison budgets, not so much milk is added as to make the brew look in any way appetising, just enough to make it muddy brown in colour. Sugar is classed as a luxury in prison and so catering departments do not waste it on prisoners. If you want sugar in your tea then you must purchase it at your own expense from the privatised canteen supplier. Some prisons now supply tea bags and powdered milk to prisoners so that they can make their own brew, but, typically, the stuff they supply is the cheapest. Prison-issue tea bags are like little parcels of tea dust wrapped in a bag that has the feel and consistency of a woolly blanket. Pop one into a cup of hot water and you can wait for up to ten minutes before the water even changes colour. And prisoners have discovered that the sachets of prison-issue powdered milk are highly flammable, which, if you are making a bomb or planning an arson, is great, but not so good for making a decent cup of tea.

Our prisons run on tea. Well, tea and heroin. But the comforting and familiar ritual of sitting down for a cup of tea with someone, especially while being held captive in the strange and unfamiliar environs of an institution like Her Majesty's Prisons, is something of the outside world that even the longest-serving prisoners hold on to. Almost every act of prison indiscipline that I was involved in over my time behind bars (and there were many) was thought out over a nice cup of tea. That's the great thing about tea: it oils the thought process. Even when you are planning subversion and mayhem, tea is perfect for that lull before the storm. If you don't believe me, just ask Charlie Bronson.

NOEL 'RAZOR' SMITH was born in London in 1960. He has a total of fifty-eight criminal convictions and so has spent the greater portion of his adult life in prison. While serving time he taught himself to read and write and is now the author of four books, the winner of several Koestler Awards and the editor of *Inside Time* magazine.

PLAYLIST

The truly tea-ish moment occurs sometime around four in the afternoon, when the day is drifting boringly towards evening and a pick-me-up is urgently required. This is often tea, but it can also be music, and it can definitely be both. ALEXIS TAYLOR of Britain's smartest pop group HOT CHIP shares six songs that put some gleetime in his teatime.

4PM ETERNAL

NEW YORK CITY — *I'm Doin' Fine Now* (1973)

When I think of 'afternoon music', I think of BBC Radio 2. My wife always has it on. New York City's 'I'm Doin' Fine Now' came on a few months ago and just jumped out at me as an amazingly forceful and uplifting pop song. Radio 2 isn't consistently right for my tastes in music (or presenters) but I do appreciate the way they will, at around

4 or 5pm, introduce me to fantastic soul and pop classics that I might otherwise have missed.

LORENZO ST DUBOIS — *Love Power* (1968)

The musical film *The Producers,* on whose soundtrack this is found, really suits teatime viewing. As satires about the Nazis go, it is a gentle one, and works well for a 4pm screening on a rainy day. Lorenzo St DuBois auditions for a role in the musical *Springtime for Hitler.* The producers, exhausted at having seen hundreds of useless wannabe Hitlers, are very much taken by LSD's impassioned performance of this song. It enlivens their afternoon, much as the soundtrack often enlivens mine.

ODETTA — *Sometimes I Feel Like a Motherless Child* (1960)

After hearing this in the Pasolini film *Il Vangelo Secondo Matteo,* I spent many afternoons in the university library searching for more information. Weeks later (these were pre-Wikipedia days), I tracked down the album and mail-ordered a copy. When I eventually listened with friends at their house in Romsey, it was great to see that my research had been worthwhile, that other people also connected with this beautiful song.

PRINCE — *The Ballad of Dorothy Parker* (1987)

I have probably listened to 'The Ballad of Dorothy Parker' in the afternoon more than any other song. Prince's ability to transport the listener to a very personal space, and to imbue a sensual story with humour, is unique. The lyrics tell a story. It's about time spent with a waitress, and getting in and out of a bubble bath fully clothed. The characters really seem to inhabit a tangible space and time. For some reason I feel like that time is the afternoon.

TIM BUCKLEY — *Blue Melody* (1969)

I got a cassette recording of Tim Buckley's *Blue Afternoon* LP, which was a rare record I was after as a teenager, from a kind man who worked in Probe Records in Liverpool. I was there visiting my girlfriend at the time. Now whenever I hear the song 'Blue Melody' from that album it brings back a vivid memory of one particular afternoon when we listened to that cassette in her bedroom. The song is pretty languid, a loose but nonetheless intense live take that I imagine took place late at night somewhere in California. But for me it will always recall a specific afternoon in Liverpool.

A TRIBE CALLED QUEST — *Bonita Applebum* (1990)

This is something I would have first heard on *Yo! MTV Raps* in the early 90s, but in fact it represents a current listening habit. My daughter and I were dancing to it yesterday at teatime and she was wondering what Q-Tip was saying — what a 'Bonita Applebum' is. I couldn't explain it very well.

ALEXIS TAYLOR, an extraordinary musician and songwriter, lives in the London borough of Haringey. He sings and plays keyboard in HOT CHIP, whose backlist, pleasingly enough, includes a song called 'Let's Tea Party'. When is your next album? we asked. We are recording it now! he answered.

THE HAPPY READER

Three stages of boiling
Photographed by JASON EVANS

80°c

THE BOOK OF TEA

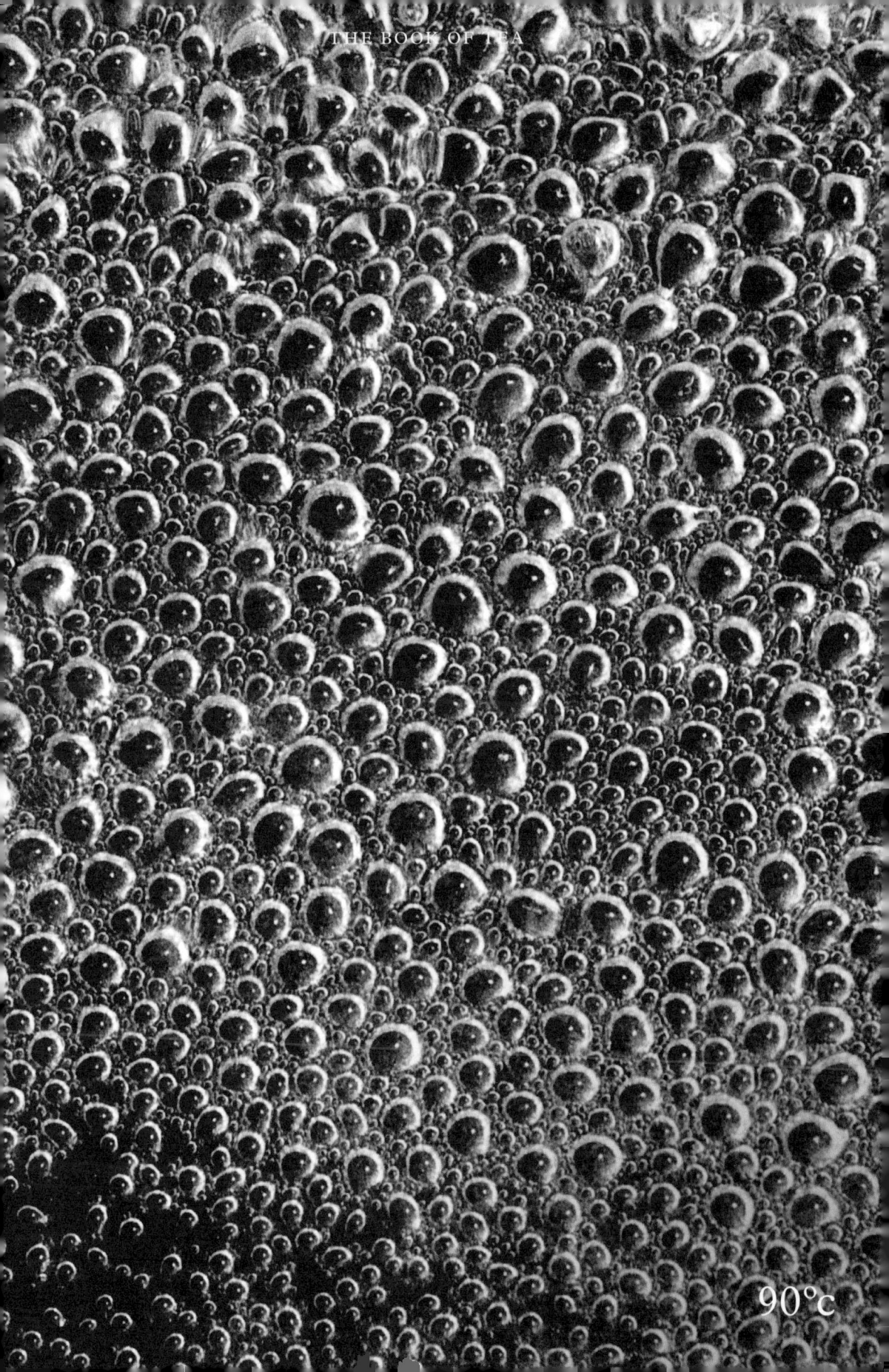

90°c

THE HAPPY READER

100°c

LETTERS

The last issue of *The Happy Reader* featured proto-detective novel *The Woman In White* and an interview with the actor Dan Stevens.

Dear Happy Reader

I enjoyed Naomi Alderman's discussion with Dan Stevens about the proliferation of lighthouses and creepy uncles in 2012's Booker-nominated novels. I wondered if they knew about the 1941 hit novel *The Snow Goose* by Paul Gallico. It centres on both a lighthouse, and a creepy-ish, uncle-ish character.

Peter Law, London

....

Sir—

When you politely gave me the tip that Norman Mailer's book collection had turned up at the Provincetown thrift store, I made it one of my first destinations when I arrived. I went straight to the thrift store to see what you were talking about. The three books I purchased were Mikal Gilmore's *Shot in the Heart* and John Cheever's *Falconer* and *Oh What a Paradise It Seems*.

Shot in the Heart is written by music journalist Mikal Gilmore about growing up with his famous brother, the killer Gary Gilmore. It is one of the most honest and compelling books about the underlining dark belly of America post WWII and a book that is the companion book to one of Norman Mailer's most revered works, *The Executioner's Song*, about Gary Gilmore's trial, life and public execution. It seemed so odd to me that I would end up with Norman's copy.

The other two books are also by one of my favourite authors, New England's John Cheever. John Cheever lived in the closet for his lifetime. He passed away some years ago but his work is even more dialled-in as one knows the life and pain Cheever suffered in living in the closet. His family would release their father's diaries in volumes which tell of his father's indiscretions. The journals of John Cheever are landmark on the closeted married suburban sexual male. I had read all his work with the exception of *Oh What a Paradise it Seems*. I was excited to have Norman's copy, Mr Napoleon Macho. I read it. I devoured it and in a token of friendship I sent the copy in the mail to my dear friend, Stephin Merritt. It seems it was left on the doorstep outside of his house. He never received it. The package was stolen and now somewhere out there is Norman's copy.

Cesar Padilla, New York

....

To whom it may concern

How interesting that Dan Stevens predicts a revival of *Iron John* but I think there's something more to the appeal of 'the wild' that *Iron John* represents than just anxieties around masculinity. Don't we all live with the sense that technology is developing at a pace so fast that our animal brains don't have enough time to process it all? As Wallace Stegner wrote in his 'Wilderness Letter': 'We simply need that wild country available to us, even if we never do more than drive to its edge and look in.' The wild reminds us that to be in control in life is not the point. The point is hope, harmony and perhaps to reclaim our sense of wonder.

Saskia Vogel, Berlin

If you have an insight or observation about the next Book of the Season or anything in this current issue, please send a letter to The Happy Reader, Penguin Books, 80 Strand, London WC2R 0RL or letters@thehappyreader.com. To be considered for the summer issue, your letter must reach us by 6 April 2015.

IN SUMMER

Our next Book of the Season takes the reader on a long, memorable Mediterranean journey: *Granite Island* by Dorothy Carrington

The summer issue of *The Happy Reader* will push out from the shores of *Granite Island: A Portrait of Corsica*, Dorothy Carrington's famed portrayal of the so-called 'scented isle'. If you'd like to be up-to-date by the time the issue arrives, you have until June, or alternatively the book will make for an entertaining, fascinating and deliriously dense beach read.

Granite Island opens with an account of the author emerging from the cabin of a boat and seeing Corsica for the first time. This was 1948, and the trip would prove more significant than she could ever have known. 'My life really ended when I set foot in Corsica,' she later reflected. 'My former role-playing ended, and my vocation began.' By the time *Granite Island* was published, in 1971, she had spent much of her life living in Ajaccio, the Corsican capital. She was enchanted by the island's mountains, forests, remote towns and even its wild air of danger, fed for years by a sense of independence unquelled by centuries of being conquered by larger neighbours. And she was mesmerised by the prehistoric statues that had stood beneath olive trees, in semi-forgotten obscurity, for millennia. As we read her masterwork, we partly want to visit Corsica, and partly feel we are already there.

ORDERS
Granite Island is available from penguinclassics.co.uk

SUBSCRIPTIONS
Subscribe to *The Happy Reader* and pay only the cost of p&p (from £8 per year) simply by visiting thehappyreader.com